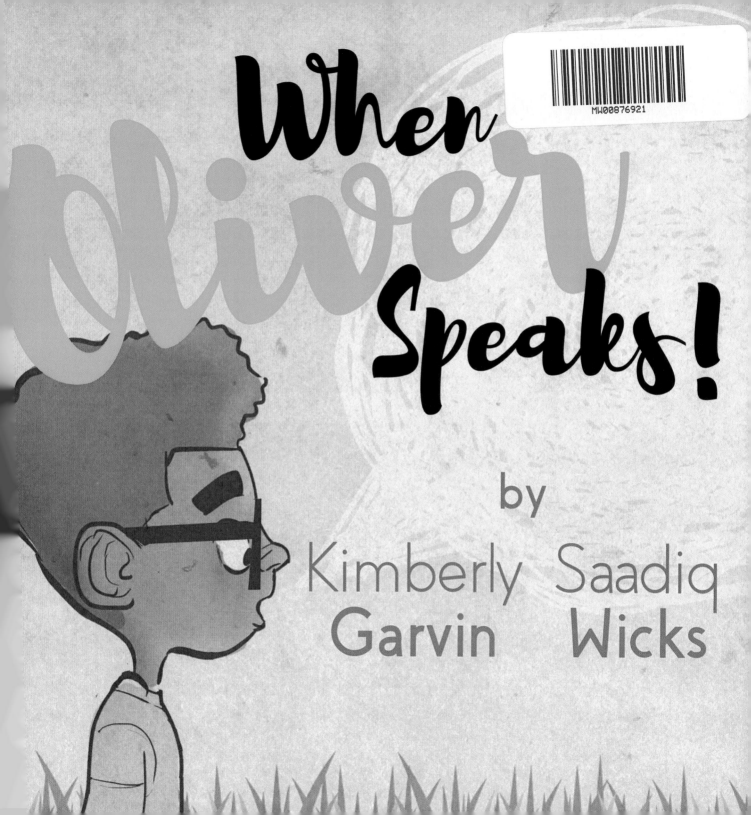

When Oliver Speaks!

by

Kimberly Saadiq
Garvin Wicks

When Oliver Speaks!

by

Kimberly **Garvin**
Saadiq **Wicks**

Design and Illustration by

anthonytyronehoward.me

"As the founder of a nonprofit focused on granting wishes for struggling and special needs children, I've met my share of "Olivers." There is nothing more difficult to witness than a child embarrassed of their disability. Oliver Speaks is a beautifully illustrated delightful read that encourages children to embrace their disabilities, inspiring them to use their uniqueness to their advantage. When Oliver Speaks is sure to empower any child facing adversity. What a powerful message!"

--Debbie Savigliano, Founder, Bianca's Kids

"When Oliver Speaks is a touching story that all children who might be nervous about speaking in front of their class, particularly those who stutter, can relate to. Oliver experiences some of the universal emotions felt by children who stutter, yet he bravely embraces his stutter as the trait that makes him unique. A wonderful read for all kids who stutter, their families, and educators alike."

--Tammy Flores, Executive Director, National Stuttering Association

"When Oliver Speaks is a wonderful book! It is honest, creative, brave, compassionate, and educational. I highly recommend this book and I wish it had been around when I was a child."

-- Taro Alexander Founder & President of SAY: The Stuttering Association for the Young

When Oliver Speaks
Copyright © 2017 by Kimberly Garvin & Saadiq Wicks

This book is a work of fiction. Names, characters, places, and incidents either are products of the author's imagination or are used fictitiously. Any resemblance to actual events or persons, living or dead, is entirely coincidental.

Editor: Hamishe Randall
Cover: 3-Sixtydesign.com
Illustration & Layout: Anthony Tyrone Howard

Ordering Information:
Quantity sales: Special discounts are available on quantity purchases by corporations, associations, and others. For details, contact:

Indigo River Publishing
3 West Garden Street Ste. 352
Pensacola, FL 32502
www.indigoriverpublishing.com

Library of Congress Control Number: 2017944864
ISBN: 978-0-9990210-1-9

First Edition

With Indigo River Publishing, you can always expect great books, strong voices, and meaningful messages. Most importantly, you'll always find...words worth reading.

Foreword

Thank you Marcus Bullock for always being there for me. Thank you, Mom for always giving me the courage to find my voice and Be Heard. Sydni...I Love YOU!

Saadiq Y. Wicks

For unto me a child was born...Thank you, Father. Saadiq it is only through your voice that I understand true courage and strength. You have an unprecedented will to do and to be, that is truly inspirational. Thank you for sharing your gift with us.

Kimberly Garvin

Meet Oliver.

Oliver is one of the most **amazing** kids you'll know – next to you, of course. He's seven years old, and like many seven year olds...

He enjoys playing **basketball**.

Oliver likes to use his **imagination**.

He enjoys reading all genres of **books**.

He likes to watch
his favorite
television show.

He even has disagreements with his **siblings**.

The one thing that
Oliver **doesn't** enjoy...

is speaking!

Oliver is a person who stutters. Stuttering is a disruption in the production of speech sounds, also called "**disfluency**"

[dis-floo-uh n-see].

This means that when he **speaks**, very often his words don't come out the way he wants them to.

Can you imagine Oliver's **anxiety** when Mrs. Bakersfield informed the class that tomorrow would be the last day for students to present their **"All About Me"** projects?

So far, Olive
had managed to
avoid presenting
Once, he'd gone to th
bathroom just a
Mrs. Bakersfield wa
about to call his nam

Another time he went to the nurse, claiming that he had horrible **stomach pains.**

Then there was the time he lucked out because of a **fire drill**.

This time, there appeared to be no getting around presenting, especially since Mrs. Bakersfield **looked directly** at Oliver when she addressed the class.

That afternoon, he went home and told his mother the **dreaded** news.

"M-mom, I-I-I-I have som s-som s-something to tell you," **Oliver said.**

"You do?" **his mother asked**

"Y-y-yes," **said Oliver.**

"Does it have anything to do with an **"All About Me"** project, Oliver?"

He replied with a grim, "Y-y-yes. **Mrs. Bakersfield** told you?"

"Yes, Oliver. Mrs. Bakersfield telephoned today and **mentioned** that perhaps you weren't feeling well.

She said that you've bee spending an awful lot o time in the **bathroom**, and in the **nurse's offic

"I-I-I-I've been hiding," **Oliver admitted**. "I don't w-w-want to do that p-p-project! I don't w-w-w-want to present in front of the c-class!

And, and, and *I don't want them to know all about me!*"

Oliver was now embarrassed and ashamed. He lowered his head.

"Y-y-yes," he whispered. **"I-I hate my st-st-stutter."**

"Sweet Oliver," his mother said. "I understand how you feel, but it's your stutter that makes you the **awesome** and **fearless** kid you are. A stutter is nothing to be ashamed of.

Your stutter is as much a part of you as your **eyes**, your **ears**, your **nose**, and your heart. Do you hate these other parts of yourself?"

Thinking, Oliver reluctantly responded, **"No."**

"And why not?" **his mother pressed**.

"Be-be-be-because w-without them
I-I-I w-wouldn't be able to s-s-s-**see**,
hear, s-s-s-**smell**, or b-b-**breathe**."

"Then try to **accept** your stutter."

"Give it a chance, just like you gave **riding your bike** a chance, **learning to read** a chance, and **getting along** with your **brother** and **sister** a chance."

"Well," Oliver began, "If I-I-I-I can get along with **them**, I-I-I-I guess I-I-I-I can get along with m-m-m-my st-st-st-**stutter**."

"W-w-will y-y-you help m-me p-p-**practice**?"
"Of course I will! And tomorrow you will be
brilliant!" his mother **beamed** with pride.

The next day, as the rest of class was settling into their seats, Oliver settled himself. He couldn't help but feel a little **nervous**, but he was ready - ready to be **brilliant**.

And, when Mrs. Bakersfield called on him, Olive didn't need to use the **bathroom**, and he didn' ask to go to the **nurse**.

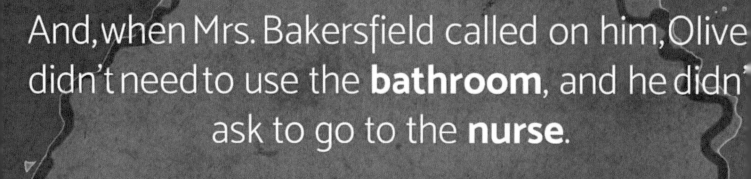

Instead he walked straight to the front of the clas carefully holding the "**All About Me**" poster he ar his mom worked on the night before.

THE END.

Made in the USA
Las Vegas, NV
16 October 2024

97006375R00026